Look Out LONDON, Here We Come!

Culture Kids Adventures

Patricia Myers

ARCHWAY
PUBLISHING

Archway Publishing books may be ordered through booksellers or by contacting:

Archway Publishing
1663 Liberty Drive
Bloomington, IN 47403
www.archwaypublishing.com
1 (888) 242-5904

ISBN: 978-1-4808-9147-0 (sc)
ISBN: 978-1-4808-9146-3 (hc)
ISBN: 978-1-4808-9148-7 (e)

Library of Congress Control Number: 2020909622

Print information available on the last page.

Archway Publishing rev. date: 7/9/2020

Dedication

This book is dedicated to my children, Joe and Katie, who became travelers from the day they were born. Their journeys varied from the "super economy" high school Europe tour (with Mom as chaperone), to Joe's China environmental exchange program, to Katie's three years working with El Salvador's poorest children.

Later, these two explorers joined me and my husband in Saudi Arabia, Bahrain, and Kuwait, where we worked for nearly a decade. Katie attended the Saudi American International School, building friendships with students from forty countries. Joe interned in Saudi, working with people from all demographics, often eating french fries and lamb, cross-legged on a plastic floor mat. Their love of travel and making friends from around the globe never ended as they crisscrossed the world over the years, happily riding camels in Egypt near the Valley of the Kings to thoughtfully walking through the remains of Pompei. Each of these experiences taught them to open their hearts and minds to all people and to see that we are equally beautiful, good, and worthy of respect.

Why London? Great Britain was always a special place for our family. Katie bought her first prom gown at London's Selfridges, and Joey will never forget his first experience with jet lag.

I also dedicate this book to our darling granddaughter Sienna, who, since she was a toddler, begged for stories about world travel. Her love of hearing about people, geography, history, and culture inspired me to write this book. I predict she will someday work at the United Nations, bringing her openness and love of everything international to the world.

This nana looks forward to exploring the world with all her grandchildren—Sienna, Beckett, Lucy, Joey, and Reed—in years to come.

Special Thanks...

Special thanks to my husband, Lou, who encouraged me to write this book and share our travel stories. He was the publishing production guru allowing me to continue with my consulting work while completing this long-wished-for project. As always, his attention to detail and commitment to quality made the book something we could both love and be proud of.

And warm appreciation to my dear friend Kathleen Logsdon, who took the time and interest to gently edit, being the forever English teacher.

Patricia Gervase Myers

Colleyville, Texas

Contents

The Best Christmas Present Ever

As the morning light seeped through the window, Sienna's eyes opened wide. No time for sleepyheads! It was Saturday, and soon Nana and Papa would arrive to take Sienna and her brother, Beckett, on their big adventure across the ocean.

Before she could hop out of bed, Beckett was tugging at her blanket and holding his favorite monkey, Mr. Zee.

He shouted into her ear, "We're going to miss our plane. I just know it! London Bridge is waiting for us, and we're going to miss our plane!"

Sienna grabbed her checklist. Suitcase packed, and carry-on almost packed. Warm socks for the airplane and her new earbuds. She checked her phone. 7:05 a.m.—just enough time to eat breakfast, dress, and be at the front door.

She bragged. "I'll be ready before you will."

With that, Beckett sped down the hall.

The next few minutes were filled with excitement and questions.

Beckett moaned. "I want to go, but I hope *everything* isn't different from how we do things here."

Sienna sighed. "Of course it will be different. But maybe it will be a *good* different."

Mom repeated what she had said before. "Just go with an open mind. Who knows. You just may learn a thing or two from a new country.

Dad said, "And knowing Papa and Nana, I'm betting you might actually have fun along the way."

Parents and grandparents exchanged last-minute reminders.

Mom kissed the kids, saying, "Remember to be polite and kind to everyone you meet in London. And if you don't like something that's offered to you, just take a little bite and thank them."

Dad gave each of them a huge bear hug and said,

"Remember that you're guests. Try your best to learn everything you can about England. And don't forget that everyone you meet will be learning about *our* country by meeting you."

"We know, we know," Sienna and Beckett said together.

Just then, the doorbell rang and Papa called, "Let's go! Your chauffeur is here."

Within seconds there was a flurry of suitcases and jackets—all tumbling down the steps—and somehow, finding their way into Papa and Nana's car. This was the day they had waited for since Christmas. Nana and Papa retired from their jobs and promised that, as a Christmas gift, they would to take Sienna and Beckett on an educational trip to a new country. Today, their big adventure was about to begin.

Sienna closed her eyes and imagined herself up, up in the clouds, gliding for thousands of miles. She pictured herself stepping off the plane onto the tiny island that she had stared at on her wall map since Christmas. England, the country the Pilgrims came from. England, the country where our first US presidents came from.

"London, England, here I come. Ready or not," she whispered to herself.

Nana told them so many things about London: Buckingham Palace, London Bridge, and the strange stones at Stonehenge.

For three months they had memorized the names of places they were going to visit. But Sienna still had butterflies in her stomach. If only she didn't have to fly three thousand miles over the Atlantic Ocean to get there. Her worried thoughts were interrupted by her little brother.

Beckett was already asking the same questions he had asked a million times. "Do you think we'll be able to go to a Manchester United soccer game? Are you sure London Bridge isn't going to fall down again?"

Sienna tried to take her mind off the long flight. "I just want to see the queen. Or at least see a real princess. That's all I really care about."

Nana laughed. "You never know. I've been there many times, and I've never been lucky enough to see Queen Elizabeth. But there are so many other wonderful things to see that it won't matter if we miss one thing on your wish list. One of *my* favorite things is enjoying a proper afternoon tea."

Papa had his own wish. "I'm still looking for the best fish and chips in London. Maybe I'll find them this trip."

Finally, they stood at the check-in desk of British Air.

"Please, Nana, I want to show my own passport," Beckett pleaded.

Sienna examined her passport with a sigh. "The only thing that looks like me is my pigtails. Ugh—I look like a baby!"

The agent examined their passports and tickets and said, "Well, Miss Sienna, you've sure grown up, young lady. But those big green eyes are a sure match."

Next, they lined up for security. They kicked off their shoes, guided their backpacks through the metal detector, and breezed through security. Soon they heard the words they were anxiously waiting for.

"British Air flight 2307 to London is now boarding." Their adventure finally began.

They fastened their seat belts, and Nana wrapped soft blankets snuggly around them. They watched *Jungle Book* on their laptops for the gazillionth time and soon went to sleep for the rest of the ten-hour flight to London.

Chapter One
Questions to Think About

- Have you ever gone on a trip without your parents? If you have, how did you feel about leaving?

- When was the first time you remember going on an airplane?

- Where did you go and why?

- What did you enjoy the most about traveling on an airplane?

- Was there anything you didn't like about traveling on an airplane?

- Have you ever traveled outside the United States?

- If you have visited another country, you have a passport with your picture and birthday on it. Why do you think you have a passport and need to show it when you leave or enter another country?

- If you haven't visited another country yet, what country would you like to visit and why?

London at Last

They landed at Heathrow Airport in rain and fog. Papa told them to always expect some rain in London.

"I'm still tired." Beckett yawned. "I kept waking up. I want to go back to sleep." He moaned.

Sienna was bleary-eyed but rubbed her face hard with her palms. She didn't want to miss a thing.

At baggage claim, she thought about petting the security dog, who was wagging its tail around her suitcase. But the stern expression on the policeman's face stopped her. The dog moved from person to person, sniffing their bags.

Papa explained, "They're looking for certain foods or plants people might bring into the country. It's important that bugs aren't on anything we carry into England. They could infect the plants here."

Nana added, "They're very careful about protecting their farms. You'll see them doing the same thing when we get back to America."

Once outside with their bags, Beckett perked up when he saw the long lines of little black taxicabs outside the departure gates. He already knew the steering wheel was on the right side of the car and that people drove on the other side of the road.

They squeezed into a taxicab and sped down the road.

"This is so weird," Beckett screeched.

"No, not weird." Papa corrected. "Just different from how we drive in America."

"Remember what Mama told us," Sienna reminded Beckett in her teacher voice. "There will be lots of different things that we'll see."

"Okay, okay," Beckett agreed. "But it still *feels* weird."

The cab pulled into the Hilton London Park Lane Hotel.

"Home sweet hotel," Nana announced.

The hotel was tall and grand, but the best part about

it was the beautiful park across the street. The park was bustling with people and lots of kids and dogs.

"I hope we get to play there," Beckett said.

"We'll see," Nana answered.

Beckett knew that meant maybe, maybe not.

Up the elevator and into room 1005.

"I get the bed by the window," Beckett shouted.

Sienna rolled her eyes. "Whatever," she muttered.

Oh no. Something strange was happening. Sienna felt dizzy and was suddenly very tired. Almost at the same time, everyone sat on the bed or sofa and looked at one another yawning.

"Jet lag." Nana moaned. "It's one thing I dislike about travel."

Papa explained that different time zones around the world meant London was now seven o'clock in the morning while Dallas was eleven o'clock at night.

Beckett yawned. "I don't care if it's morning in London. I want to go to bed."

Sienna hated agreeing, but she whispered, "Me too."

"We have to try to stay up a few more hours so we get on London time," Nana warned.

None of them got much sleep on the flight, so she was just as tired as everyone else. Within a few minutes, her idea drifted into thin air. Beckett was sound asleep on Papa's lap, and Sienna snuggled up on the pull-out sofa. Soon everyone was fast asleep on their first day in London, England.

Chapter Two
Questions to Think About

- When Sienna and Beckett arrived in London, there was a special dog sniffing their luggage for fruits and vegetables that passengers may have brought on board. Nana told them each country must make sure that certain insects and bacteria living on fruits and vegetables aren't carried into the country to protect the food being grown there. Why do you think this would be a good idea?

- Did you know that in some countries, cars are driven on the other side of the road than we drive our cars on in the United States? What do you think your parents would think about this?

- Have you ever heard of jet lag? What causes it?

- Sienna, Beckett, Nana, and Papa all need to get used to the different time of day in London. How do you think you would feel if this happened to you?

- Have you stayed in a hotel? What's the most fun thing about staying in a hotel?

Hello, London!

Finally, everyone was awake and ready to explore. Nana drank her coffee and Papa checked his emails.

Sienna realized she and her brother had fallen asleep in their travel clothes!

Nana knew what they were thinking. "Even I was too tired to help you get into your pajamas, so don't even think about wearing those clothes again today!"

Beckett giggled. That was *exactly* what he was thinking. He wondered how Nana always read his mind.

After quick showers, they all headed to the restaurant on the first floor of the hotel. They were starving. Papa asked the waiter if they still served breakfast food.

Sienna waited patiently to announce her favorite joke. "What does Frosty the Snowman eat for breakfast?"

Beckett shouted, "Frosted Flakes!"

Papa laughed out loud, even though he had heard it many times before.

But Sienna frowned and jabbed Beckett on the arm. "That's my joke. Get your own." She growled.

Not to be outdone, Beckett asked, "What did the egg do when it saw the frying pan?"

Sienna quickly jumped in. "It scrambled!"

"Hey!" Beckett frowned. "Let Papa and Nana answer!"

Papa broke up the "almost-argument." "Come on, kids, let's order our first British food. What will it be? Toads in the hole or black pudding?"

"Huh?" Beckett shouted. "What's a toad in the hole?"

"Well, it says it's sausages in a casserole. Sounds good to me." Papa said. "I'm ordering that. No Cheerios or scrambled eggs while *I'm* in London."

The waiter poured tea for everyone.

Sienna began to protest, but Beckett whispered, "Let's have tea with lots of cream and sugar!"

They weren't usually allowed to have tea at home, but it seemed impolite not to drink it here. Nana and

Papa seemed to ignore the heaps of sugar and honey the children poured in.

"Yum," Beckett said. "I'm just like a London person."

Nana corrected him, "You're just like a Londoner—but with a little too much sugar and honey, that is."

At that moment, the mystery food was served. Beckett expected the toads to be jumping out of the casserole. But the waiter explained that the little sausages just *looked* like they were peeping out of the sauce, and that's how it got its name. That made more sense than live toads being served for breakfast. Still, Beckett closed his eyes with his first bite. It was hard to think about what might have been a toad.

With their first meal over, Papa directed everyone outside to the corner where they waited for the right bus. Not any bus. A big blue double-decker bus. They hopped on, headed to the top level, and adjusted their earphones Papa brought to listen to the guided tour describing each famous place they passed. The next stop was London Bridge.

"Did it really fall down?" Sienna asked.

Papa, who knows everything about history, seemed happy to answer that question. "Most people agree that the bridge we're walking on has fallen down a few times. But each time, it's been rebuilt. People say that hundreds of years ago, it was pulled down, because it was made of ropes and wood. Later, it was built to be stronger, but a huge ice storm made it fall down."

This made Beckett a little nervous. He stared at the huge arches above him.

Papa laughed. "Don't worry. Today, it's super strong. It's built from concrete and steel. I'll bet there are a million people, cars, buses, and trucks all crossing at the same time. It must be pretty sturdy for that!"

Just then, the tour bus beeped its horn, and they all hopped back on for the next stop.

"Where to next?" Sienna asked. "I really, really want to see a princess!"

Nana sighed. "Remember, honey, the chance of seeing a real princess is slim, even here in London. But we're heading to a place where kings, queens, princes, and princesses lived for hundreds of years."

Beckett squinted as he looked at the picture of Buckingham Palace in his guidebook. "I thought those guys were only in fairy tales and on TV. There aren't real ones, are there?"

Sienna hated to hear this question, because she wasn't sure queens and princesses were real, either.

Nana answered in a flash. "Oh yes. There are hundreds of kings, queens, princes, and princesses. There are duchesses, dukes, countesses, and counts. They're all members of real royal families."

Sienna was relieved to hear Nana's answer.

Beckett thought a minute. "And knights of the round table too?"

Papa jumped into the conversation. "Well, knights are special royalty. In the old days, a king or queen chose people who became knights to protect the country. I think that's what you're talking about."

Beckett didn't care about princesses. He hoped they would meet knights in armor at Buckingham Palace.

They walked down a long street. Dozens of red and blue flags waved in the breeze on each side of the street. Each flag had a giant X.

Soon the palace came into sight. Huge metal fencing surrounded it. The area was packed with tourists. Sienna and Beckett wished they were a little younger, so Papa could put them on his shoulders to get a good look. With a little patience, they wriggled up to the fencing for a better view.

Something was about to happen. They could feel it. Soon, horses led the way for a marching band–trumpets, trombones, clarinets, cymbals, and drums. Then came the Queen's Guard—all in exactly the same uniform: bright red jackets with huge black fur hats and shiny swords hanging by their sides. They marched in straight lines.

Beckett jumped for joy. "Now this is London," he happily shouted. "Look at that sword. It has to be ten feet long!"

Papa quickly corrected him, saying, "Well, not quite that long, but you can be sure that these are real soldiers. As the Queen's Guard, those swords are real *and sharp*!"

Sienna spotted the flag holder. "I love that flag with the big X. I want to buy one to take home."

"This is what England is really all about," Nana said. "It has so much history and so many interesting things that have been done exactly the same way for hundreds of years. It's called tradition."

Papa added, "Did you know this country is about 1700 years old? America isn't even three hundred years old. You could say our country is a baby if you compare it to Great Britain."

Beckett scrunched his nose. "I'm confused. Nana calls this country England, and you just called it Great Britain. Which is it?""That's a great question," Papa said. "Because it's a very old country, it's had many changes in its life. The country we're in today is England. But the countries that are attached to it and part of their government are Wales and Scotland. The whole group is called Great Britain."

"That makes a little more sense, but it's still confusing," Beckett admitted.

"So are the queen and king and prince and everybody who lives here in charge of all three countries?" Sienna asked.

Nana said, "Well, that gets even more confusing. Yes, the royal family is the honorary head of the countries. But just like our country, people vote for who they want to really rule the country."

Papa knew the children were getting a lot of new information. "Don't worry, you'll learn more and more about London this week."

Sienna thought about the castle and the king and queen

who lived there. "I'm wondering where the king and queen are right now."

Nana looked at Papa and whispered to him, "Do you think I should tell her?"

"Tell me what?" Sienna demanded.

Nana took her hand and said softly, "I don't want to get you more confused, but here in England, there can only be one king or one queen serving at a time. It's not like all the fairy tales we read, where there's a king *and* queen."

"Oh no," Sienna cried, "I don't want to hear this! I think there should always be a king and queen together."

"Well, that's just the way it is in this country," Nana said. "Royal families have always been complicated, but someday we'll go to a country where there *is* a king *and* a queen."

Just then, there was a loud commotion and sirens screeched close by. The crowd was cheering. They heard someone say, "Look, it's the royal motorcade."

Nana asked a tour guide what was about to happen. He told her the queen was going to the Chelsea Flower Show this morning.

He smiled. "If you're lucky, you might catch a glimpse of her."

Everyone was pushed back into a straight line to allow the fancy cars to pass. One car had lots of flags, and from inside, a grandmotherly looking woman waved her white gloves at the crowd.

Sienna and Beckett waved back.

Nana laughed. "Guess what? You've just seen the queen!"

"But Nana, she had a hat on. Where was her crown?" Sienna asked.

Nana knew she was surprised. "I think you're going to have to find the kind of princesses you're looking for in your books and in the movies. Queens wear their crown for important occasions, but now, they're a lot like we are. They wear modern clothes and live their days a lot like we do."

Sienna was a little disappointed. She had come all this way and saw no crown or gowns. At least she saw a real live castle, and according to Nana and Papa, she waved to a real live queen.

Chapter Three
Questions to Think About

- After reading this chapter, what have you learned about Sienna?

- How would you describe Beckett?

- Have you ever been to a restaurant or someone's home and ate something that was brand new to you? Were you surprised at how it tasted—good or bad?

- What is your idea of what a queen or king would look like today?

- How do you think Sienna felt when she saw her first real queen and she looked more like a grandmother than what we read about and see pictures of in our fairy-tale books?

Stonehenge: The Mystery of Great Britain

The next few days were busy, busy, busy. They saw the London Eye, one of the oldest and tallest Ferris wheels in the world.

"I really wanted to ride it," Beckett said. "Too bad we couldn't get tickets."

Papa had a pretty good idea that it was a bit too scary for all of them. "Yes," he agreed, "I'm sure we all would have loved being four hundred feet up in the air—*especially Nana.*"

Nana gave him a knowing look.

"I wonder if we could see *The Lion King*," Sienna said

wistfully. "I don't think I'm going to like seeing some big rocks in the middle of nowhere."

Papa disagreed. "Even if you don't like rocks, I think you'll enjoy the train ride to Salisbury and then, Stonehenge. Let's give it a chance. We'll hail this taxi."

The cab driver sounded very different from the other drivers. "I'm from Scotland," he announced. "And where are all of you lovely people from?"

When the children told him they were from Dallas, Texas, he shrieked. "Oh, my goodness gravy! So where are your boots and cowboy hats?"

Papa got a good laugh from that. He explained that he left them at home. "I thought they wouldn't fit in over here." Papa chuckled.

Beckett couldn't remember him wearing a cowboy hat except to the rodeo one year. And he *never* wore cowboy boots.

But Nana just put her finger on his lips. "Let Papa have his fun," she whispered.

Soon, they pulled up to Waterloo Station where hundreds of people were moving in every possible direction.

"Let's check the split-flap board showing train

schedules so we can catch the next train," Papa shouted over the noise.

Sienna wanted to ask him why the driver thought he was a cowboy just because they lived in Texas, but she didn't have time right now. They bought the tickets and lined up for the next train.

"Darn," Papa complained. "They changed the train schedule board to a computerized one. The old split-flap ones were so much more interesting."

Nana gently scolded him. "Oh, Papa, I'm sure the new one is even more accurate. You know we have to make way for progress."

"I guess so," Papa said, a bit sadly. Papa was very high-tech, but he still loved some of the old equipment that he considered beautiful.

Trains packed with passengers came and went. It looked like people from every corner of the world were going to other corners of the world. Men in white robes that looked like pajamas read newspapers. Women with scarves covering their heads pushed strollers. Children with brightly colored shirts that matched their hats ate ice cream cones, and a group of teenagers with purple hair sang and played a flute, drum, and tambourine.

"Wow," Beckett exclaimed. "I feel like I'm walking around a globe!"

"That's a very creative thought," Nana answered. "We're just four sets of feet traveling around this great big busy world."

This was not at all what the children thought Londoners would look like.

Once they boarded the train, they bought black currant fizzie, that tasted like cherry soda, and vanilla wafer cookies for their two-hour trip.

Small villages with houses and stores whizzed past. As they moved further out of London, they saw more goats and sheep than they ever saw in Texas.

This reminded Sienna to ask Papa about his conversation with the taxicab driver. "Why did he think you were a cowboy, Papa?"

"Such a good question, Sienna. People who have never been to another country always have funny ideas about people who live there. Sometimes, they only see a television program or a movie about that part of the world. It makes them think that all the people must be just like the movies. Our taxicab friend probably saw a western movie or read a book about Texas. So that idea stuck in his mind."

Nana added, "This is why we love taking you to different places in the world. You'll see different people for yourself. You'll also figure out that people may look different and dress differently and eat different foods. But most people just want to enjoy their families and be happy, no matter where they live."

Beckett looked around the train. Nana was right. Mothers and fathers played with their kids. Young people and old people were reading, listening to music, or using their tablets or phones.

"Yup," Beckett decided. "We might look different, but inside, we're probably a lot the same."

Just then, they felt the train slow down and they heard the announcement. The loudspeaker blared, "Arriving at Salisbury Station."

Sienna didn't see any huge rocks around. It looked like a quaint little village with shops and places to eat. There were lots of souvenirs, so she figured they were close to Stonehenge. Papa told them that Stonehenge was the oldest construction in England. Archeologists thought it could be five thousand years old.

"How many stories high is it?" Beckett asked. He was becoming more interested because he loved buildings.

Papa laughed. "Oh no, it's not a building. It's just huge rocks. Some of them are on top of each other, all arranged in a circle."

Sienna scrunched her nose. "What's the big deal about that? I could put stones on top of each other in a circle!"

"Not if they weighed tons and tons," Nana reminded her. "Look over there. That's Stonehenge right in front of us."

As they got closer, Sienna realized her bragging was pretty silly. The sign said the huge stones were thirteen feet high and seventeen feet wide. And yes, the rocks weighed more than twenty-five tons—that's fifty thousand pounds!

"Well, that doesn't look so hard to me," Beckett said, as he stared at the simple circle of stones. "A good construction crane could do that with no problem."

"Is that so?" Grandpa teased. "So, when do you think cranes and pulleys were invented?" Beckett and Sienna didn't have a clue. "Let me tell you. They were invented hundreds of years *after* these rocks were placed here."

Sienna listened carefully as she stared at the gigantic stones. She couldn't even imagine what five thousand years were and who the people were who built Stonehenge. "Hmm. So how do you know when these rocks were really put here, Papa? Especially since it was so long ago?"

Papa was looking at the information booklet about Stonehenge and read from a page. "Scientists now have a way of figuring out the age of almost anything on earth. They use a process called carbon testing. And these tests tell them the age of the rocks. They also found five thousand-year-old bones inside the circle. So Stonehenge might have been used as a cemetery."

What seemed like a boring trip to see rocks became much more interesting! They walked under the arches made of stones—*five thousand* years ago! They sat on the grass to listen to a young man explain more about this strange place.

"I'm Elliott. I'm an archeology student at Durham University." Sienna knew that archeology was about digging up and studying rocks and very old things. "Thousands of scientists and archeologists worked hard to find out why this place was built. No one completely agrees. It could have been to look at stars and planets, maybe even to figure out when things were going to happen—like an eclipse of the moon. But they didn't leave anything written, so we'll never know for sure."

Elliott thought for a minute and then said, "Stonehenge will always be a mystery, even to scientists."

"Wow!" Beckett shouted. "This is so cool. The Mystery of Great Britain!"

Nana was just about to tell him to whisper. But the crowd cheered and repeated what Beckett said. "Hurray for the Mystery of Great Britain! Hurray for the Mystery of Great Britain!"

Sienna glared. "Show off," she whispered. But she was excited about this mystery, too.

Elliott was delighted that Sienna and Beckett were now so interested. "Would you like to see how people lived thousands of years ago?"

"Yes, yes," they quickly replied.

Excitedly, they followed him down a narrow path. It looked like a miniature village, the kind you put around a Christmas tree. He explained that the houses were built to match what archeologists thought people lived in thousands of years ago. In one area, straw was being cut into long pieces. In another area, mud and straw were being chopped up and mixed together for the walls.

"Who are these workers?" Papa asked.

Elliott explained that they were archeology students

who studied ancient houses. They were building the tiny huts as part of their studies.

Sienna watched a group of busy students. They were crushing what looked like hunks of white chalk into the mud mixture.

"Do you think we could help?" she asked.

"Why not?" Elliott laughed.

A girl with a face mask called Sienna over to her. The girl's blue jeans and T-shirt were covered in white dust. "Here, put this mask on and start smashing the chalk until it turns into powder."

Nana wasn't so sure about this, but Sienna was having too much fun to stop her.

Elliott explained, "This chalk is really limestone. It's dug from mines around here. Nowadays, they have equipment to crush and form the kind of chalk we use today. But we try to do things just as they must have done it centuries ago."

Beckett was already helping another group of students lay out the straw pieces to tie together for the roof. "Look, Elliott, I'm building a house!" Beckett yelled. "This is so much fun."

"Well, it's fun when you just have to do it for a little

while," Elliott reminded him. "But it was hard work to do it for many weeks to make one roof. Let's go inside to see what life was like five thousand years ago."

Inside, Sienna asked, "So whose room is this?"

Elliott smiled. "It's where the whole family lived. This room is where they cooked, ate, slept, and played."

Mats were spread out on the ground with woven blankets and some bowls and pots.

Elliott added, "And the fire pit is there to cook on and keep the family warm."

The room was no bigger than Sienna and Beckett's bedrooms in Dallas.

Nana smiled. "It's tiny, but I'm sure there was a lot of togetherness."

Beckett looked around and thought for a minute. "Well, all I can say is, I hope they all liked each other."

Everyone laughed.

Back on the bus to the train station, they couldn't stop talking about the mysterious rocks and the tiny houses. They boarded the train at Salisbury Station for their journey back to London.

"Five thousand years of history is a lot to see in one day," Papa said, as he snuggled up with Beckett.

The train moved, jerking forward, but no one felt it. By this time, all four were sound asleep.

Chapter Four
Questions to Think About

- When Papa told the cabdriver he was from Dallas, Texas, the driver thought he was a cowboy. Why do you think he thought that?

- As Beckett walked through the train station, he said, "I feel like I'm walking around a globe." What do you think he meant when he said this?

- If you saw huge rocks that were as high as buildings sitting in the middle of a field, how would think they got there?

- The little houses that people lived in thousands of years ago had one room for the entire family. What do you think would be difficult about that?

- Can you think of anything that would be good about your entire family living in one room?

Art, and Fish and Chips

When Sienna and Beckett woke the next morning, they didn't remember being tucked into bed the night before. They were pretty tired after their journey five thousand years back in time. Nana and Papa had carried them to their hotel room and put their pajamas on.

The rain pounded against the window, and it was chilly in their pretty blue room. They pulled the covers up and were ready for cartoons. Instead, they heard the chatter of English accents and the morning weather report.

"Rain is expected later today, so don't forget your brolly," the weatherman reminded. Even Nana, who knew most of the local words, didn't know what a brolly was.

"Maybe it's a raincoat," Papa guessed.

"Let's look it up on your phone," Beckett suggested.

"Well, I was pretty close," Papa announced. "It says a brolly is an umbrella. I guess we figured out that it had something to do with the rain."

Beckett chimed in, "That's a really silly name for an umbrella, but whatever. Let's remember to bring our brollies." He marched around the room with his open umbrella, nearly poking Sienna in the eye.

"Okay, okay, Mr. Beckett," Papa scolded, as Sienna shoved Beckett away. "No brollies or umbrellas, or whatever they call them, open in the room! Now let's have a quick breakfast so we can get to the museum before the crowds."

Only two days left in London, and Beckett wasn't thrilled about spending it inside an art museum. "I'd rather go to the zoo," he moaned. "They have a white-necked monkey."

Papa agreed with Beckett, but he had already promised Nana that they could spend one day at *her* favorite place— London National Gallery. Maybe the zoo would be on tomorrow's schedule.

On their way to the restaurant, Papa announced that in England, Yorkshire pudding is a favorite breakfast.

"Pudding for breakfast?" Beckett was surprised. "Sounds good to me."

Sienna stuck with scrambled eggs and fruit.

"I'd still order something like eggs or cereal to go along with your 'pudding,'" Nana said with a little chuckle.

After the waiter brought the food, he asked if Beckett was ready for his Yorkshire pudding. Beckett saw Nana wink at Papa. He wondered what the joke was. The waiter carried a little silver tray and placed it right in front of Beckett.

"Your Yorkshire pudding, sir."

Beckett was confused. "Hey, this isn't pudding—it's a biscuit."

Nana and Papa laughed out loud and the waiter giggled. "I'm sorry, sir. We seemed to have played a little prank on you. This little puffed-up biscuit is what we call Yorkshire pudding. It got its name so long ago, even my grandmother can't remember why we still call it pudding."

Beckett didn't see what was funny about it. He was still waiting for pudding for breakfast. Preferably chocolate. This definitely wasn't what he had in mind.

He growled at Nana and Papa, who were still giggling at the little joke, but he decided to fill the crust with strawberry jam. It wasn't chocolate or vanilla, but it was really tasty!

"I guess this will be another thing I learned about England," he said, as he gobbled up his little pretend pudding.

Just then, the front desk manager came in to tell Nana and Papa that their taxicab was waiting. They rushed out, waving at the waiter. Now everyone in the restaurant was laughing about the little Yorkshire pudding joke.

This time, their taxicab driver was from Ireland. "I came here as a lad," he said. "And I still go back to my homeland a few times a year."

"How far is Ireland from here?" Sienna asked politely. She was hoping it was close so they could visit.

"If you drive to the other side of the country, it's just a short flight over the water to Dublin. That's the capital of Ireland."

Nana added, "You could compare it to trips we've taken in the United States. It would be something like flying from Dallas to California to see your cousins."

Beckett was surprised. "So you can go from one country to another in the same time we go from one state to another state? I guess *our* country *is* really big!"

Papa thought for a minute. "I'm guessing that England is about half the size of California. That gives you an idea."

"Wow," Beckett exclaimed. "For a little country, England sure has a lot of interesting things to see and do."

Nana was the first to see the sign: London National Gallery. She was thrilled. "One of my favorite places in London! Every time I come here, I notice something I didn't see before."

Beckett wondered why an art gallery would be so special to Nana.

"I have to say that I agree with Nana," Papa said.

So Papa loved it too? Now Beckett was even more confused.

Sienna looked at the big, beautiful building. She was sure *she'd* like a museum full of paintings. She loved the Kimbell Museum nearby their home in Fort Worth. She tugged on Nana's jacket. "This looks like a pretty old building. So how can you see *different* things every time you're here, Nana?"

Nana smiled. "Some of my favorite paintings are here, and I've seen them many times. But every time I see them, I notice something different or new about them. I see a detail that I never saw before. It's almost as though my eyes get better with every visit."

Sienna and Beckett saw that Nana *and* Papa were excited to walk through the huge doors. They always knew Nana and Papa loved art, but they didn't really understand what she meant about her eyes getting better every time she came.

They were happily surprised when a young woman asked if they wanted to play a special scavenger hunt game while they were in the museum. She had a name tag and the word "docent" on her jacket. Papa pointed to the word and explained to the children that a docent was a person who knew a lot about the museum and could guide them around and answer questions.

"But, Papa," Beckett blurted out in a loud voice, "she said scavenger hunt! So that means we don't just have to go around looking at paintings!"

Nana gave him a look that Beckett knew very well. The look said for him to lower his voice.

The woman who was the docent smiled and explained, "Here's a list of things to find in the paintings in each wing of the museum. Just check it off when you see it. And answer all the questions."

This sounded easy and sort of fun. "Oh, I almost forgot," she added. "There are prizes at the end of your visit if you can find everything on the list."

"Whoa, this is more like it." Sienna bragged. "For sure, I'm going to win."

The woman continued. "Sorry, but you have to do the game in teams, so you both either win or lose—together."

Beckett crossed his arms but announced, "Okay, I guess we can both win. Let's get going."

Since Nana and Papa knew the museum, they helped the children look in each gallery. The first item on the list in Room A was finding "a bouquet of pink flowers." The children moved from painting to painting. Some they liked, and some pictures they didn't like at all. They came to a painting of a mother and a baby.

Sienna spotted it first. "I see them. I see them. Pink flowers."

Nana explained that this was one of her favorite paintings because the artist drew what he thought Jesus and his mother would have looked like. "This mother looks like every other mother in the world—loving her baby with all her heart and showing him flowers—maybe even showing how to smell them. This painting warms my heart."

The children looked at the mom and her baby and agreed with Nana.

"This could be our mom," Sienna said. "She's so pretty."

Beckett agreed but then examined the painting more closely. He added thoughtfully, "Well, it could be. But if that were me in the painting, I wish they would have put more clothes on me."

All the people who were near them laughed out loud. Beckett was a little embarrassed.

Papa explained that this was how they painted years ago. "It was just their style. But I agree with you. If it were painted today, you might have a little baby outfit on!"

Nana laughed.

Papa asked about the details of the questions in their booklet.

"We have to write the name of the painting, the artist, and when it was painted," Beckett read.

They weren't allowed to get too close to the paintings because they were so old and valuable. Papa put his glasses on and squinted, reading the small sign next to the painting. "The name of it is *The Madonna of the Pinks,* and the artist is Raphael. Can you guess when it was painted?"

"I'll say a hundred years ago," Beckett guessed.

"I'm thinking it was done fifty years ago, because it's in perfect condition," Sienna argued.

"You're both way off," Papa announced. "It was painted more than five hundred years ago."

Beckett examined it more closely. "Wow! How do they get it to look so good after all that time?"

Nana reminded them about the special equipment used to tell the age of the rocks at Stonehenge. "They have scientists working with artists to figure out the age of the paintings. They clean and restore them, so they can be enjoyed for many years to come."

"Yes," Papa added, "and they use a special X-ray machine called radiography. They look underneath the paint to see if there might be another painting. Maybe the artist painted over one he wasn't pleased with."

"So if they made a mistake, they could paint right over it," Beckett figured. "That's smart."

"Yes, that's very possible," Papa agreed.

This museum visit was going to be a lot more interesting than they thought. They were beginning to understand what Nana said about her eyes getting better every time she came here.

"Let's hurry up and get to the next room," Sienna urged.

They walked from room to room, discovering so many interesting things about the paintings on their list. For one painting, they had to guess what the artist might have been *thinking* when he painted it. It was a picture of ballet dancers.

"This painting was done by a man named Degas," Nana told them.

Sienna examined the card under the painting. "It's called *Ballet Dancers*. It looks like his name is "Di-gas," not "Day-gah.""

"Ugh," Beckett said, "I don't care what his name is. I hate ballet. It looks like she's rubbing her foot because it hurts."

Nana stepped back and stared at Beckett. "Is that what you really thought when you looked at this painting?" She looked very surprised.

Beckett wasn't sure if Nana was mad or glad. Or if he

should change his story. "Well, they *could* be having fun, but maybe not," he stammered.

Nana beamed and shook his hand. "You are now officially an art expert."

Beckett was proud but not sure what he said that was so smart.

Nana continued. "Many people say this artist was thrilled with the ballet. And he loved the beautiful way they danced and moved. But other people agree with you. They say his painting shows how painful and difficult ballet could be for these dancers."

"Hey, Papa," Beckett boasted. "I'm smart about art! Smart about art!"

Sienna glared. "Well, I disagree. I think the painting is about how beautiful they are, and how good they are at dancing. I think she's adjusting her shoe, not rubbing her foot. So there!"

Papa interrupted. "Hey, guys, remember, this is a team project. You've just figured out what the best thing about art is. You can decide for yourself what you think is wonderful and what you don't like at all. And you can decide what it's really about. You both did a great job thinking about this piece of art work. Congratulations, art lovers!"

Finally, after three hours, they finished each question in their scavenger hunt. Everyone was excited. Papa and Nana found their favorite paintings, and Sienna and Beckett began to know what they liked and didn't like.

"I think I know what you mean about your eyes getting better." Sienna hugged Nana. "I think *my* eyes have really improved since I walked in the front door."

They proudly took their art game booklet to the gift shop where they turned it in, wondering what the prize was. The sales woman was impressed! She told them they could each choose a poster of their favorite painting as a special gift from the museum.

This decision was much harder than they could have imagined. Nana's choice was a painting of a lady standing by the water, called *The Morning Walk*. Papa decided on a picture of an old ship being brought into shore by a tugboat. It was called *The Fighting Temeraire*. The woman told him he had good taste, because it was one of the most popular boat paintings.

Papa laughed and told her the real reason he chose it wasn't because of the boat. "I love the beautiful clouds in this painting and always wanted to paint a sky like this. Maybe this will inspire me," he said wishfully.

Then it was Sienna's turn. "I made my choice. At first, I was going to pick this painting because there was a big crowd around it so I thought it had to be famous. But then, when I got up close to see it myself, it made me happy." It was the well-known painting by van Gogh called *Sunflowers.*

Nana complimented Sienna's choice. "Wonderful selection, honey. Van Gogh is one of the most famous artists in the world."

"Oh darn," Beckett said with a grumpy face. "You stole my artist. My picture was painted by that guy too. I picked this picture of a little yellow chair sitting all alone in someone's kitchen. And, guess what? It's called *Van Gogh's Chair.*"

The sales lady smiled. "Oh my, young man, you've chosen a very interesting piece of art."

Sienna rolled her eyes. "Oh, here we go again."

Beckett beamed and waited for the rest of the story from the museum clerk.

"This painting was done when van Gogh was angry with another famous artist because the two of them had such different ideas about art. It was van Gogh's way of saying, 'This simple chair is my kind of art.' There are lots of stories about this piece, sir."

Beckett felt very smart and special. "Wow! Who would think I'd become an art expert in one day?"

By this time, Sienna *had* to laugh about Beckett's newfound love of art.

Papa gave her a wink and said, "You and Nana always loved art. Isn't it nice that your brother now has an appreciation for the finer things in life?"

Sienna winked back at Papa and asked that her sunflower poster be put in a cardboard tube to keep it from bending when she took it on the plane. "I can't wait to frame it for my room," she whispered. "I now own a van Gogh painting!"

Everyone was delighted with their art but very tired after visiting the National Gallery of London that morning.

Sienna pulled out her crumpled list of "Things to Do in London." She happily checked off the art museum. "Oh, no, Papa, I'm so sorry. Only one more day in London and we still haven't—"

"Shush. I'm thinking," Papa said as he closed his eyes. "I'm thinking, I'm thinking. What haven't we done yet?"

Before he could say another word, Beckett shrieked. "I know, I know! Papa is still looking for the best fish and chips in the world. We need to help vote on that!"

By this time, everyone was starving, so the idea was a great one. Without saying a word, Papa hailed a taxicab.

Sienna was surprised. "How can we take a cab if we don't know where we're going?"

"Aha," Papa said," We're going to find that out when we get in the cab."

Before the driver could ask where they were going, Papa announced, "Please take us to the best fish and chips restaurant in all of London."

"Well, sir," the driver answered. "It won't be in any of these fancy-dancy hotels in the middle of the city. I would suggest Golden Union for the best chippies in the city. My family took me there as a boy. It's not that far."

"Onward," Papa agreed.

The cab squirmed out of the traffic, and soon they were surrounded by the amazing smell of fresh fried fish. The cabbie introduced Papa to the owner, who seated everyone and handed out menus.

"May I tell you a bit about what makes us special?" the owner asked. Everyone nodded. "Our fish is fresh each day from the Atlantic, and we buy only the best cod and haddock. You also might want to try some creamy mushy peas to go along with your chippies. My mum's recipe is still the best in London," he bragged.

By this time, Beckett could eat a whale, not just a little fish. Beckett smacked his menu on the table and said, "So what are we waiting for? Let's do it."

Sienna and Beckett ordered plain fish and chips. Nana and Papa insisted they all share a creamy mushy pea order and a chicken and mushroom pie, which sounded terrible to Sienna and Beckett.

"I know, I know, we have to try British food. But I'll just take a tiny bite. I want to save room for my chippies." Beckett laughed.

Sienna piped in. "I can't wait to get back to school and tell my cafeteria lady that I'd like the chippies."

Papa had another view. "Once you taste these, I have a feeling the ones we have in Texas won't compare. And remember, I've tried fish and chips all over London for many years. You all get a vote, but *my* vote is the important one."

Within minutes, their fish and chips (which were like

fat French fries) and fresh tartar sauce was served. Then, came a huge bottle of vinegar.

"What's that for?" Sienna asked. "We're not having a salad."

Nana opened the bottle. "Another favorite of mine— vinegar on my chips."

"Yuck," both children said at the same time.

"You won't know until you try it," Nana said as she smothered her chips with vinegar.

Sienna got her courage up. "Okay, I'll try one. Hmm— not bad." She ate another and another chip from Nana's plate.

"Hold on there, girly. If you like them, here's the vinegar." Nana passed her the bottle.

Beckett wouldn't admit it, but he copied Sienna when she tried things, especially new food. He got up his courage to try vinegar on one chippie. Then another. "I like it, but I'll stick to my ketchup."

They tried the mushy peas and chicken and mushroom pie but both made a face.

Papa wasn't saying a word. He stared into his plate,

popping a large bite of fish into his mouth and closing his eyes as he slowly chewed.

"Well," he finally announced, "I think we hit the jackpot. This is outstanding. Crispy on the outside and light and fluffy on the inside. Perfecto! As the English would say, it's jolly good."

Sienna and Beckett cheered. "Hip, hip, hurray for the best fish and chips in the world."

They dived into their plates, leaving the mushy peas and pie to Nana and Papa, who loved them.

Chapter Five
Questions to Think About

- Why was Beckett so surprised that his breakfast was a little biscuit?

- If your grandparents told you that you were going to an art museum, what would you think of that idea?

- If you were Beckett or Sienna, what do you think would be the best part of visiting The National Gallery in London?

- What do you think is the best part of doing art projects?

- Have you ever tasted fish and chips? What do you think made these fish and chips in this story so special?

The Not-So-Ordinary London Zoo Visit

When the children woke, they were a little sad. This was the last full day of their London trip. The time flew by, and they would soon be back to the United States, where fish and chips would be replaced by cheeseburgers and french fries. In his head, Beckett prepared his reasons for why they should visit the zoo.

But Sienna was faster with her speech. She stood at attention. "I know you want us to always be learning, right? The London Zoo is one of the world's top zoos. It would be very educational."

Beckett was just about to interrupt, but she quickly continued.

"Our brochure says they have lots of animals on the world endangered species list."

Beckett's ears perked up. "What does that mean?"

Papa explained that some animals in the world were becoming very rare. "They might not even exist if zoos like this one didn't protect them," he said thoughtfully.

Beckett asked, "You mean like how the dinosaurs are all gone now?"

"Exactly." Papa nodded.

Everyone looked at Nana. She was the deciding vote. "I'd love to visit the zoo. That is, as long as we can be back for afternoon tea."

Nana wasn't selfish, but everyone knew she had her heart set on taking the children to the Dorchester Hotel for afternoon tea, whatever that meant. This was the hotel where she took Beckett and Sienna's mother and Uncle Joe when they were teenagers.

"I think you deserve that little part of our trip," Sienna said sincerely, as she gave Nana a hug. "Besides, even *I* want to see what's so special about having tea at a hotel."

Beckett wasn't going to be outdone. He gave Nana a huge kiss and said sweetly, "I think the trip to the zoo will be just what we need to prepare for your big tea party."

Nana was a pushover for his charm, and Papa just winked at all of them.

"Case closed," Papa announced. "Onward to the London Zoo. But we'd better hurry. We can get breakfast from a street vendor before we catch a taxicab."

Once they were out on the street, Nana and Papa ordered an egg sandwich. Sienna and Beckett chose ham and pickle sandwiches, which they thought sounded interesting. Papa also ordered a bag of cream-filled doughnuts, even though Nana gave him a frown.

They ate their breakfast in the taxicab while the driver told them a little about the famous London Zoo. The children discovered the cab drivers were wonderful tour guides. Most of them lived in London all their lives, so they knew everything you could wonder about. He gave them a pamphlet to read while they ate the not-so-healthy, but delicious, breakfast.

"Whoa, look at this lemur. It looks *crazy!*" Beckett pointed to a wild-looking animal with huge eyes.

Sienna was fascinated by the pictures of a pool where penguins were swimming. "They're just so cute! I can't wait to see a penguin in person. I know I saw them in

San Antonio when I was five years old, but I don't really remember much."

Before they could read the rest of the booklet, they reached the zoo entrance. A large sign caught everyone's attention. *Sleepover at the Lion Lodge.*

"Can we, can we?" Sienna and Beckett begged.

Nana and Papa were glad this was their last day in London, so they didn't have to make that decision.

Papa smiled. "Wow, a sleepover at the Lion Lodge. Sounds fascinating."

Nana quickly jumped in saying, "Unfortunately, we won't have time to sleep over at the Lion Lodge on this trip." She gave Papa a *look* to stop him from saying anything more.

But Papa winked at Nana and continued. "I sure wish we could have slept with the lions. Maybe next time!"

Sienna and Beckett hugged Papa—he was always ready for a new adventure!

Nana walked away, mumbling, "I'll get our tickets while you three dream about sleeping with lions."

From the gorilla house to the lion lodge, the zoo was everything they hoped for. They stopped at the education building to hear a talk by the head zookeeper, Mr. Hardwick. He explained what the letters Z S L stood for, on the signs around the zoo. The letters meant Zoological Society of London.

"This zoo works hard to find and house the animals, insects, birds, and amphibians that need special care and attention for them to have babies and grow in numbers," he announced.

The zookeeper asked the audience where they were from. Most people were from England. When he heard that Sienna and Beckett were from Dallas, he asked them to stop and see him after his presentation.

The children wondered if he was going to give them a little button or sticker of the zoo, but it was much better than that!

"Did you know we have a special children's program here at the zoo?" he whispered to the children. "It's called zookeeper for a day."

As he started explaining the program, the children's eyes lit up. But when he said it was tomorrow, everything changed. They remembered that today was their last day in London.

"I guess we won't be able to do that," Beckett glumly replied. "We're on our way home tomorrow."

The zookeeper thought for a minute and announced, "Well, how about if we make it *zookeeper for an hour or two*? You've come a long way to visit us. We want this trip to be as special as we can make it."

Sienna and Beckett jumped up and down. Nana and Papa were surprised. But mostly, they were a little worried about what it meant to be a zookeeper for a day—or even an hour.

Mr. Hardwick gave each of them a green-striped apron, heavy gloves, and rubber boot they put on over their shoes.

"Let's get started on some of my daily duties. First, we'll check in on the giraffes. They're such gentle, easygoing animals."

The children were allowed to hand feed the tall, beautiful animals. Sienna fed carrots and special vitamin biscuits to a baby giraffe. Beckett fed the taller giraffes acacia leaves that Mr. Hardwick told them came from Africa. Then the zookeeper asked them to help clean out one of the empty monkey cages.

"Hmm, this isn't my favorite part of the job," Beckett admitted.

"Yes, that's true," Mr. Hardwick agreed, "but sometimes, stinky work goes along with the fun parts."

The last job they helped with was feeding the penguins. This was definitely an exciting job. Sienna had a bucket of live fish while Beckett had a large tray of very smelly sardines. The penguins took the food right from their hands.

"I think I'm going to smell like a fish all day," Sienna said as she tried to quickly empty her bucket.

"Good work." Mr. Hardwick congratulated them. "You are both fantastic honorary London zookeepers."

His assistant carefully printed their names on a certificate he put in a large envelope with *The London Zoological Society* printed on the outside. The children cleaned up with special antibiotic soaps in the employee washrooms. One more amazing story to share with their parents.

"Do you think Mom and Dad will ever believe us when we tell them what we did?" Sienna wondered.

"Oh, don't worry," Papa said. "I've got every second of this in pictures to prove it!"

Mr. Hardwick handed them his card. "I'd love to see those pictures if you could send me an email."

They all hugged Mr. Hardwick and thanked him again for being so kind. Even Nana and Papa could hardly believe they had this amazing experience. What a great new English friend!

Several cabs were lined up at the zoo entrance. They hopped into the first one in line.

"Yuk! You smell like a monkey." Sienna pushed Beckett away.

Beckett held his nose, pushing his face into Nana's sweater. "Gross! You smell like a sardine."

They didn't have to read Nana's mind. This was *not* going to be a day they skipped a shower. She pretended to hold her nose and sniffed. "I'm not sure if I smell monkeys, penguins, or giraffes. But you are all going to smell like soap before we go to afternoon tea!"

Chapter Six
Questions to Think About

- One of the animals the London zoo housed was the endangered lemur. Why do you think that some animals are in danger of being extinct from our planet?

- Do you know of any animals that are now extinct that you wish were still alive in the world?

- What part of being a zookeeper for a few hours would you enjoy the most?

- What would you enjoy the least?

- Why do you think Mr. Hardwick, the zookeeper, chose Beckett and Sienna to help him that day?

Nana's Choice: Afternoon Tea

With showers finished, they all agreed they were starving—as usual.

"Are we going to lunch first?" Beckett asked. "Tea isn't going to fill me up. I need some pizza or at least some chippies."

Nana gave him a stern look, saying, "Excuse me?" But she didn't really mean "excuse me." She was really saying she didn't like the tone of what he said.

Beckett said, "Sorry, Nana. I just meant that I don't understand why we aren't going to lunch before we go for your afternoon tea."

Papa cut in. "I think we should all just go along

with Nana's request. Trust me, I don't think we'll be disappointed or hungry either."

They went down the elevator and, once again, into the taxicab to what Nana called "the *famous* Dorchester Hotel."

Inside the lobby, Sienna twirled around, doing a little ballet dance. "Wow, this is like a castle. Look at the crystal lights and pretty furniture."

Nana was thrilled that Sienna already noticed how beautiful the hotel was. "This isn't even the fanciest hotel in London, but I think their tea is elegant and very traditional."

Papa translated for Nana. "That means it's very 'London' and has been done this way for quite a long time."

Beckett was still totally confused. He thought, *Tea is tea. What's so special about all this?* He didn't dare say what he was thinking out loud.

Nana took Sienna's hand. "Shall we, Princess Sienna?"

Beckett jumped right in and grabbed Papa's hand. "I guess that makes us princes or kings, right, Pops?"

Papa chuckled and spun Beckett around before walking into the tea room.

They were seated in a large, beautiful room around a little table filled with white napkins and lots of silver spoons and knives. The waiter was dressed in a tuxedo and soon delivered a huge silver tray of sandwiches. Papa and Nana ordered champagne, and the waiter brought Sienna and Beckett tall champagne glasses filled with sparkling water and several cherries.

Beckett lifted his glass and toasted Papa. In a very loud voice, he shouted, "Now this is living!"

At first, Nana looked shocked. But when the rest of the people in the room laughed and toasted Beckett, she smiled too. Beckett always seemed to get away with the funny things he said. Mostly because they *were* funny.

The sandwiches were rather tiny, but they all looked delicious. They each agreed to try different ones and give their opinion. They compared the descriptions from the menu to figure out what they were. Papa enjoyed the smoked salmon, and Nana's favorite was the cucumber with mint cream cheese. Sienna loved the egg salad, and Beckett gobbled down five chicken sandwiches in a few minutes. He didn't even mind the fancy mustard that the waiter told him was something called pommery sauce.

Sienna pretended to be a princess and was talking with

a London accent. "I would just adore these in my lunches every day," Sienna announced wishfully.

"You sound like you have a sore throat," Beckett said between bites.

"I think she sounds royal," Papa said as he patted her head. "I wish I had a little tiara to put on you. It would fit this room perfectly."

Beckett was a little jealous. He held up his glass and said in his best English accent, "I think this girl sounds like a fake princess. I happen to know she's from Texas!"

Papa messed up his hair and asked, "Well, what if we made you a knight and Sienna a princess. Would that fix things?"

Beckett giggled. "Only if I got a real sword!"

Nana ended the argument, saying, "When we're having afternoon tea, we're all royal family, so let's just enjoy every minute of our fantasy."

The waiter poured more tea water for everyone. The teas weren't just little paper bags, like they were at home. Some were tiny silk bags of tea, and some were crushed-up tea leaves placed in a little strainer on top of the tea pots. Nana and Papa seemed to enjoy the tea as much as the champagne.

Sienna and Beckett tried different teas, all with lots of honey. But they also had the most delicious chocolate milk they ever tasted. Just when the sandwich tray was taken, another silver tray of cookies, cakes, and scones was delivered. Sienna and Beckett enjoyed scones from a Starbuck's near their house, but these were quite different. Puffy and moist.

The waiter named each of the fancy treats. Some names they had heard before, and others were very different. Coconut macaroons, hobnobs, orange flower tea cakes, and banana eclairs. They finally understood why Nana loved afternoon tea!

Nana and Papa were both surprised when the waiter brought an ice cream and sorbet cart to the table. Another silver tray of waffle cones, ready to be filled, soon appeared.

Even Nana thought this was a fine finish! "This isn't the way I've always had afternoon tea. But this new little twist makes it even more perfect!"

Everyone agreed.

"So, Beckett, do you think we need to stop for pizza on the way back to the hotel?" Papa teased.

Beckett was finishing the last of the scones in one hand and licking his ice cream cone with the other. "Nope. I think I'm good for now, but I wonder if they have a doggie bag for me to take home."

Even Sienna laughed at this idea.

They took a long last look around the beautiful room and listened to one more song being played by the pianist. As they walked to the lobby, the tea room manager presented each of them with a box of chocolate-dipped coconut macaroons.

"I wrapped them all up with cellophane so you can take them home," he politely said, with a little bow. With this, every one of them- Papa, Nana, Sienna and Beckett-felt like they really were kings and queens, princesses and princes or maybe even a knight in shining armor.

Chapter Seven
Questions to Think About

- Why do you think Beckett wasn't excited about going to afternoon tea?

- Why do you think Sienna was so looking forward to going with Nana and Papa?

- Can you think of a time when you thought something wasn't going to be fun and it turned out to be a lot of fun?

- If you were Beckett or Sienna, what do you think you would enjoy the most about going to this fancy place for afternoon tea?

- Why do you think Sienna and Beckett felt like they were really kings and queens or princes and princesses?

Where to Next?

Was it possible? Was their trip to England, the United Kingdom, the British Isles, and any other name it's called really over? Who would have thought that one vacation could include castles, endangered animals, five thousand-year-old stones, priceless paintings, fish and chips, and elegant afternoon teas? This was not at all what Sienna and Beckett had expected.

The lights in their room went out, and they fell asleep thinking of different things.

Sienna still wondered about the queen who wore a hat. Beckett thought about the baby giraffe. Papa thought about those delicious fish and chippies, and Nana tried to remember how she might make the special scones when she got home.

The alarm blared, and the morning sun came all too fast.

"I'm still tired." Sienna yawned. "The night *before* we left for England, I couldn't sleep because I was wondering what England was going to be like. Last night, all I could think about was what I would tell Mom and Dad about first!"

Beckett piped in. "Well, my favorite part was—"

Papa cut him off and said, "Don't tell us now. I can't wait to share all our favorite things about London. But the cab will be here soon."

Once in the elevator, Sienna thought about all the people from around the world who had stayed at this hotel. "I wonder if the queen has ever been in this elevator."

"It's very possible," Papa answered. "This hotel has been around a long, long time!"

Nana and Papa lived at the hotel for a few months many years ago when they were working in other countries.

"This brings back such wonderful memories." Nana thoughtfully sighed as she looked around the lobby. "I just can't stop thinking about how special this country is, and the wonderful differences from the United States. You can look at a million pictures, but you'll never really understand until you visit it, meet people, and experience its treasures."

Beckett agreed. "We read all about this country, but you don't really get it until you're right smack in the middle of it."

Papa gave him a hug. "That's so, so true, young man. And so smart of you to see that."

They waved goodbye to the front desk manager and the bellmen who had helped them all week.

Sienna stopped on the sidewalk and threw her arms into the air. "Thank you, London, for the best trip of my entire life!"

They hopped into the cab with the steering wheel on the right, driving down the left side of the street.

"It's funny," Beckett said quietly. "I thought this driving thing was weird when I got here. But now I think it's just plain different. Not weird at all."

They passed beautiful Hyde Park where children played, people walked their dogs, and teenagers tossed frisbees.

Sienna added thoughtfully, "Yes, different, but a lot the same. I'll bet people come to our country and at first think we're the ones who are different and maybe even a little weird."

Nana and Papa didn't say a word. They just looked at each other and smiled.

As they made their way to Heathrow Airport, Papa asked them to think about what their favorite part of the trip was. This was one time when Sienna, Beckett, Nana, and Papa each had a very different idea.

Sienna was sure that her visit to the London Gallery changed her idea about old museums forever. "Well, maybe the museum is tied with seeing a real castle and a real queen," she finally decided.

"If she gets two choices, then so do I," Beckett insisted. Beckett's favorite was helping build an ancient house at Stonehenge. "That was the most educational thing I did. But being an honorary zookeeper was absolutely the most fun, for sure," he added.

No one was surprised that Nana still loved her afternoon tea.

Before Papa could answer, both children giggled. Sienna announced, "We know for sure what Papa's favorite thing was–finding the best fish and chips in London."

Papa thought for a minute and announced his own

answer. "I did enjoy my fish and chippies. But what I loved the most was watching you both see the things that make this country special. Traveling is so much better than anything you can ever buy at a store. This trip won't get old. It won't get too small for you. It won't ever get lost or taken away. You'll have this adventure in your minds and hearts forever."

Nana agreed. "I think that traveling makes us all a little bit different than before we left. Remember when I said that every time I went to the museum, I thought my eyes got better? Traveling is the same thing. Your eyes get better as you see and do new things."

Of course Beckett had the last word. "It's like getting new glasses."

They boarded their plane to Dallas, and after getting tucked in for a long trip ahead, Sienna tugged at Papa's sweater. "Papa, I do have one more question. Where are we going on our next adventure?"

Chapter Eight
Questions to Think About

- Sienna and Beckett had a lot of different experiences in London. What did you think was the most interesting thing they did or saw?

- Beckett said he thought some things were weird when he first arrived in London but changed his mind after a few days. Did you ever first think something that was different from anything you saw or knew about was weird—but later changed your mind?

- Sienna wondered if people coming to the United States for the first time would think many things were strange and different. What would you tell someone who visited the United States for the first time to make him or her feel at home?

- Why did Papa say that their trip was better than any present they could buy?

- Nana said that "your eyes get better" when you see and do new things." What do you think she really meant?

NOTES

NOTES

NOTES

NOTES

NOTES

NOTES

NOTES

NOTES

Questions to answer after reading
Look out London, Here We Come!

- What did you think was the best part about reading this book?

- What was the most interesting place or thing in the book that you enjoyed hearing about and wished you could see or do?

- Was there any place or thing that the children in the story did that wasn't very interesting?

- Was it fun to meet Sienna and Beckett?

- How would you describe each child in a few words?

  Beckett:

  Sienna:

- Did you really feel like you were in London with them, seeing the things they saw and doing the things they did? How would you like to live in London?

- Did the story make you want to follow in their footsteps and travel to other countries? What other countries do you think would be interesting to visit?

About the Author

Although Patricia Myers was raised in farm country in southern New York state, her love for travel began when she packed a grocery bag of clothes to stay with any family member offering a casual invitation.

Beginning with an English degree, she worked in banking, telecommunications, and corporate relations for a Fortune 50 company, writing award-winning annual reports and speeches. With her husband, Lou, she worked in the Middle East in leadership and talent management and earned a degree in clinical organizational psychology from INSEAD in France.

Through the years, they have traveled to more than forty countries, confirming their belief that people around the world are more alike than different and all are deserving of respect and understanding of their unique cultures.

From the people she worked with in Nigeria, to her consulting team she loved in Cairo, to the colleagues who became family in Saudi Arabia, Patricia encourages people of all nations to travel. She believes it's the only way to fully acknowledge that one way of life is no better than another, as long as there's freedom to lovingly raise your family, opportunities to work to your full potential, and the ability to worship God openly.

She's currently a leadership coach in Dallas, Texas, and when not working, cares for her grandchildren and mentors young women. And she travels!

To connect with her, email culturekidstx@gmail.com

CPSIA information can be obtained
at www.ICGtesting.com
Printed in the USA
LVHW092002110820
662716LV00006B/285